FGHIJK
QRSTU
ABCDE
LMNOP

I love Florida

an ABC adventure

Sandra Magsamen

Florida is filled with fantastic and beautiful things to see and do. Just follow the **A, B, C's,** there is an amazing adventure waiting for you!

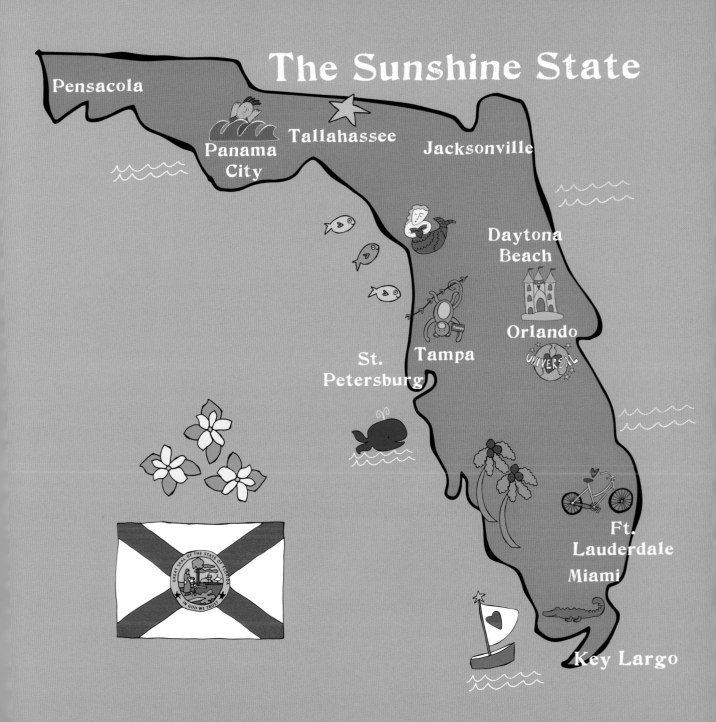

A is for **Amelia Island.**

Let's build sandcastles that reach for the sky.

B is for **Busch Gardens.**

These roller coasters make us feel like we can fly!

C is for **Clearwater Aquarium**, where we get up close to sea creatures great and small.

D is for **Disney World.** You can meet Mickey Mouse and all his friends. You're sure to have a ball!

E

is for **Everglades National Park.** Look out for a manatee or a crocodile!

F

is for

Ft. Lauderdale.

Visit Stranahan House and bike the Riverwalk for a while.

G is for the **Glazer Children's Museum,**

where we always have a blast.

Glazer Children's Museum

H is for the Miami Heat,

whose players pass the ball so fast!

I is for **ice cream cones.**

Gobble them up on a hot and sunny day.

J

is for **jumping** through the waves at Panama City Beach. Hooray!

K is for **Key West**, where we love watching the beautiful boats sail by.

L is for **Lowry Park Zoo.** Watch monkeys swing on branches low and high.

Tampa

M

is for the mockingbird.

Our state bird has a sweet and lovely song we all adore.

N is for Naples.

The Nature Center protects the sea turtles, mangroves and more!

O is for the **orange blossom.**

Our pretty state flower Smells delicious.

P is for our **palm trees.** Their coconuts are tasty and nutritious.

Q is for **quietly** gazing at the stars that shine over Jacksonville at night.

R is for running down Sanibel Beach. Its sand is oh so soft, clean and bright.

S is for SeaWorld, where Shamu always puts on a show that brings a big cheer!

T is for Tallahassee,

our beautiful state capital that we hold dear.

beach
parks
gardens
museums
fishing

U is for Universal Studios.

UNIVERSAL

Adventure is waiting for us all around.

V

is for "Viva Florida!"

All over our state there's something special to be found.

Viva Florida!

W is for Weeki Wachee Springs.

Come and see a super mermaid show!

X is for XOXO

XOXO

'cause Florida is the best state we know!

Y is for yummy

seafood like crabs and clams. They're super good eats!

Z is for the **Zucchini** Festival and its healthy, tasty treats.

adventure

an end,
can go
A and
again!

Sandra Magsamen is a best-selling and award-winning artist, author and designer whose meaningful and message-driven art has touched millions of lives, one heart at a time. She loves to travel and has had many awesome adventures around the world. For now, she lives happily and artfully in Vermont with her family and their dog, Olive.

A big thank you to my amazing studio team of Hannah Barry and Karen Botti. Their creativity, research tenacity and spirit of adventure have been invaluable as we crafted the ABC adventure series.

Sandra Magsamen

Text and illustrations © 2016 Hanny Girl Productions, Inc. www.sandramagsamen.com
Exclusively represented by Mixed Media Group, Inc. NY, NY.
Cover and internal design © 2016 by Sandra Magsamen

Published by Sourcebooks Jabberwocky, an imprint of Sourcebooks, Inc.
P.O. Box 4410, Naperville, Illinois 60567-4410
(630) 961-3900
Fax: (630) 961-2168
www.sourcebooks.com

Library of Congress Cataloging-in-Publication data is on file with the publisher.

Source of Production: Leo Paper, Heshan City, Guangdong Province, China.
Date of Production: November 2015.
Run Number: 5004883

Printed and bound in China.
LEO 10 9 8 7 6 5 4 3 2 1

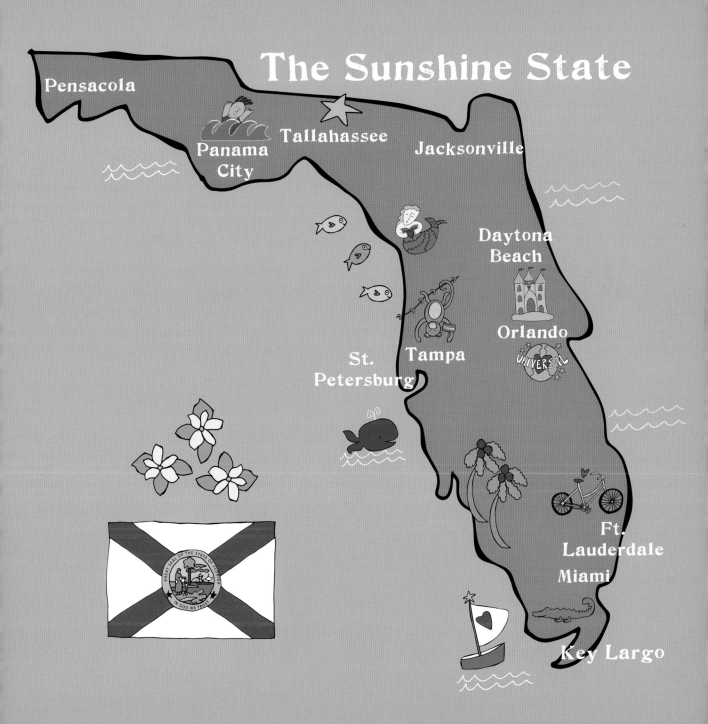

ABCDE

LMNOP

VWXYZ

FGHIJK